Interracial entertainment industry *it* couple Sasha Williams and Drake Lancaster are still going strong. Her impeccable publicist skills have kept him on the A-list, helping Drake land the lead role in a major Valentine's Day movie. When filming wraps, the couple plan on heading to Cabo San Lucas, inviting both their families along to meet for the first time.

But plans go astray when Drake reverts back to his bad boy ways during filming and gets into a huge altercation with the director. He's booted from the movie and replaced by Mitch Morrison, a hot young African-American actor who's recently taken Hollywood by storm.

While Drake struggles to repair his image, Mitch hires Sasha to help manage his burgeoning career. The move infuriates Drake, but Sasha insists it's a great business opportunity. She doesn't realize Drake's threatened by Mitch's good looks and charismatic personality and is worried the pair will bond over their African-American heritage.

The stress of it all puts a strain on the couple's relationship, especially when Mitch admits to Sasha that he's developed feelings for her and she realizes the sentiments may be mutual. With the pressures of Sasha and Drake's rocky union continuing to mount, the anticipation of their families meeting, and Sasha's elusive affections towards Mitch, the couple can't help but wonder whether their once booming relationship is about to crash. In the end, they must figure out whether their love is strong enough to withstand these challenges and carry them through this Valentine's Day.

My Unconditional Valentine
Copyright © 2019 Denise N. Wheatley
ISBN: 978-1-4874-2427-5
Cover art by Martine Jardin

Published by eXtasy Books Inc or
Devine Destinies, an imprint of eXtasy Books Inc

Look for us online at:
www.eXtasybooks.com or www.devinedestinies.com

My Unconditional Valentine
The Holiday Chronicles
Book 2

By

Denise N. Wheatley

DEDICATION

To my Baby Love, who inspires my ability to write romance . . .

CHAPTER ONE

Sasha sighed deeply and rolled over, smiling happily while eyeing the palm trees swaying outside her bedroom window. She giggled at the touch of Drake's hand playfully pinching her ass.

"Round three?" he suggested, cuddling up next to her while nuzzling her ear.

"Babe, you're gonna wear me out," Sasha insisted, glancing at her phone. "And you're going to make me late."

"I know, I know. I just can't get enough of you, gorgeous." Drake planted a soft kiss on Sasha's lips and hopped up, then threw on his jeans. "I need to get moving, too. I don't want to be late for this audition that I absolutely should not have to go on . . ."

Sasha rolled her eyes and climbed out of bed, running her hand over Drake's rippling abs on the way to the bathroom. "The sarcasm in your tone is so strong that I can actually smell it. You already know why you have to audition for this movie."

"No, I don't. All I know is that my last three films killed it at the box office. And I just hit almost ten million followers on *Instagram*. Not to mention the kick-ass appearances I made on all the late-night talk shows last month. Or—"

"Okay, okay, I get it." Sasha laughed, plugging in her flat-iron, then turning on the shower. "You're the hottest thing in the streets. But you're auditioning for Gary Rosen, hun. *The* Gary Rosen. He's one of the most legendary directors in the business. And he doesn't forget things easily."

Drake sauntered into the bathroom, his taut biceps bulging through his fitted white tee. Sasha resisted the urge to pull him into the shower and take him up on that offer of a round three.

"You don't think he's holding my days of being a bad boy against me, do you? I mean, I've completely turned my life around. I've stayed out of trouble, worked hard, and proven myself with every role I've earned. Seriously, what more do I need to do?"

"Knock your audition out the park today," Sasha replied, stepping into the shower. "That's what you need to do. Because unfortunately, while you and plenty of other people have forgotten about your checkered past, Gary hasn't. When I called and practically begged him to consider you for this part, he brought up that altercation you had with your crazed group of fans at the Hollywood Hills Resort."

"But that shit happened forever ago," Drake exclaimed, throwing his hands in the air. "Dude, get over it."

Sasha closed her eyes and let the warm water hit the back of her neck, choosing her words wisely before speaking up. "Baby, I know this is frustrating, because you've definitely reached a point in your career where you shouldn't have to audition for roles. However, you're going out for the lead in what's sure to be a huge box-office hit, and you'll be part of a star-studded ensemble cast."

"Is it going to get me an Oscar?"

"I doubt it, because romantic comedies usually don't garner awards of that stature. *People's Choice*? Maybe. But you never know, this part could lead to a role that *will* win you an Oscar. In the meantime, enjoy the great experience, a big opening weekend close to Valentine's Day, and the huge paycheck that comes along with it."

"Yeah, I guess all that does sound good," Drake responded, his eyes widening as she stepped out of the shower naked. "I don't like the fact that this movie is going to be filming all the way in New York, though. How can I be away from my girl for that long?"

"The weeks of filming will fly by, and you'll be home before you know it. While you're gone, I can finally start planning our Valentine's Day vacation. Are we sure we still want to invite our parents so they can meet? Or did we make that decision after an epic lovemaking session, when we were still high off of endorphins and adrenaline?"

Drake leaned against the wall and let out a loud belly laugh, then stared at Sasha intently as she began applying her makeup. "We were both fully in our right minds when we made the decision to invite our parents to Cabo. This thing between us? This is real, Sasha. I'm not going anywhere. So our parents need to get acquainted as soon as possible, because as far as I'm concerned, we're in it for the long haul."

"Aw, you're the sweetest, babe. And I couldn't agree more. I'll start looking at resorts and sending out emails to everyone with some potential dates. In the meantime, you'd better get going. I don't want you to be late, and I'm meeting with my boss, Nick, as soon as I get to the office to give him an update on my press event schedule."

"Are we still on for dinner tonight?"

"Of course. Now go break a leg and prove to Gary Rosen that your days of being a naughty rascal are over."

"Yes, ma'am." Drake grabbed Sasha by the waist and licked her nipple.

It hardened immediately. "Scratch that." She giggled. "You're most certainly still a naughty rascal."

"*Your* naughty rascal," Drake said. "Okay, I'm leaving. On my way to claim the role of Cliff Bailey in my blockbuster hit movie, *On Bended Knee*."

"That's right, claim it like it's already yours. Call me as

soon as you're done and let me know how it went."

"You know I will. Have a great day, sweetheart."

Drake and Sasha and exchanged one last lingering kiss before he left. She quickly slipped into a lavender mini shift dress, slid on a pair of nude patent stilettoes, grabbed her designer tote, and was out the door.

Sasha sped away from her Beverly Hills bungalow and headed towards Santa Monica Boulevard. She glanced down at the clock, wondering whether she'd have time to pick up her signature iced macchiato laced with three shots of espresso on the way to the office. But when she checked her navigation system, she saw nothing but red lines running from her current location all the way to her Century City office.

"Damn you, LA traffic," she mumbled, commanding her phone to dial her assistant, Lori. She picked up on the first ring.

"Good morning, Kline and Associates. How may I help you?"

"Hey, Lori, it's Sasha."

"Good morning," she chirped. "What's up?"

"I'm running a bit behind and don't want to be late for my meeting with Nick. Would you mind picking up—"

"An iced macchiato with three shots of espresso?" Lori interjected cheerily before Sasha could finish.

"Yes, please, you're the best."

"No problem. It'll be on your desk when you get here."

"Great. And my presentation for today's meeting?"

"It's on your chair. Organized by date and includes all of your clients' projects and press events scheduled for the upcoming year."

"Why do I even bother following up with you when you're always two steps ahead of me?" Sasha asked. "Just know that you're appreciated."

"I do, and I appreciate you, too. I'll go grab your coffee now. See you soon."

Sasha disconnected the call and lightly tapped the accelerator, continuing to crawl through the slow-moving traffic. In spite of possibly being late for her meeting, she was in a great mood and couldn't wait to tell Nick she'd gotten Drake an audition with Gary, who'd assumed she couldn't pull it off.

Gary was known for firing A-list actors on the spot over the most frivolous reasons, and any disruptions to his shooting schedule were not tolerated. But Sasha was convinced that Drake had turned over a new leaf and his days of being difficult to work with were well behind him.

She made a sharp left turn onto Avenue of the Stars and tore down the street, quickly pulling in front of the sleek high-rise that housed Kline &Associates. She hopped out of the car and tossed her keys to the valet, waving hello before scurrying towards the revolving door.

"Have a good day, Misses Williams," Reggie called out, chuckling while watching her make a run for it.

"You, too!" Sasha waved.

She jetted to the elevator and made it through the doors of the agency just in time for her meeting. When Lori saw her tearing down the hallway, she jumped up from her desk.

"Here's your coffee, and here are your presentations. I made a copy for Nick as well." Lori reached out and grabbed Sasha's tote. "I'll put this in your office. Nick is already waiting for you in the conference room."

"You're a lifesaver. Thank you." Sasha took the coffee and presentations, then hurried over to the other side of the office.

"Good morning," she panted, entering the room and taking a seat across from Nick.

His assistant, David, was sitting in the corner, clutching his laptop.

"Hey, good morning," Nick replied. "I don't have much time because today is parent-teacher conference at my kid's school and my wife is insisting that I go. So let's see what you've got."

"Okay, this won't take long." Sasha handed Nick a copy of the presentation. "As you know, my client roster is overflowing with Hollywood's top talent. I've been working with their agents and managers to help secure career-changing auditions and book roles that will really catapult their careers. And the upcoming year is filled with high-powered press tours and junkets. It's all laid out in the presentation."

Nick nodded while flipping through the pages, his eyes lighting up as he read. "This looks great, Sasha. Do you think you have room to sign on any new talent, or are you completely swamped?"

"I'm pretty booked up, but if someone extraordinary were to come along, I'd have a hard time saying no. However, it would take a really special person to get a yes out of me."

"Understood," Nick said. "Well, you've got what looks to be quite a successful year ahead of you. I can't wait to see what comes of all this. I'll review your presentation further when I'm back in the office. And on that note, I'd better get going. Parental duty calls."

"Sounds good. Oh, and by the way, you'll be happy to know that I got Drake an audition with Gary Rosen for his upcoming Valentine's Day movie, *On Bended Knee.*"

"*Wait,*" Nick's assistant David blurted out from the back of the room. "Drake Lancaster actually has to audition?"

When Sasha and Nick turned to him with raised eyebrows, David cowered.

"Oh . . . sor . . . sorry," he sputtered. "I probably shouldn't have said that. I just . . . I thought Mr. Lancaster was at a point in his career where he didn't have to audition anymore. I thought he could just—"

"Um, David?" Nick interrupted. "That'll be all. Please be sure to type up the notes from this meeting and email them to me. Thank you."

"Yes, sir," David muttered, jumping up from his chair and rushing towards the door. "Sorry again for butting in."

Nick squinted at David, then turned to Sasha. "So you were able to get our number one guy in front of the notorious Gary Rosen, huh. How the hell did you pull that off?"

"I just sweet-talked him, basically." Sasha smiled, resisting the urge to reach around and pat herself on the back. "He doesn't know we're dating, but I did tell him that Drake and I have spent a lot of time together since we signed him, and he really has turned his life around. I explained that he's taking his career very seriously, which is why his latest films have been so successful."

"Good job," Nick chimed in.

"Thanks. But while I was able to convince Gary that Drake would be perfect for this movie, I couldn't persuade him to let Drake bypass the auditioning process."

"Yeah, well, that's just Gary's way of humbling Drake and reminding him who's boss."

"I figured as much," Sasha said, following Nick out of the conference room. "But it's all good. Gary is loyal. Once you're in, you're in and can play in practically every movie he makes. So today's audition is just a small piece of a huge puzzle of success."

"See, that's why I named you partner." Nick smiled. "Keep up the excellent work. And now that I'm officially late, I'm outta here. Let me know how the audition goes."

"Will do." Sasha exhaled, glad her meeting had gone so well. She headed to her office, giving Lori a thumbs-up on the way. Once inside, she sat back in her chair, sipping her coffee and staring out at the gorgeous mountain view.

When Sasha's cell phone vibrated, she practically flipped over onto the floor trying to grab it. She hoped Drake was calling to tell her about his audition. But it was her office cohort and good friend Amanda, texting to ask if she was still available for their usual Niçoise salads and Bellinis at the Parisian Hotel's rooftop restaurant.

Sasha texted Amanda back, letting her know she was free and would meet her at *Nourriture Exquise* at noon. She added that she couldn't wait to catch her up on the meeting with Nick as well as Drake's audition with Gary.

Amanda replied immediately, saying she looked forward to hearing all about it.

Sasha turned to her computer and pulled up her email, scrolling through the messages and opening the most pressing ones first. In between sending responses, she sipped her coffee and eagerly checked her phone, waiting with bated breath to hear from Drake.

After spending the entire morning clearing out her inbox and returning phone calls, Sasha looked at the clock. It was already eleven-forty. She still hadn't heard from Drake.

This isn't good. She grabbed her tote and phone, checking it one more time to see if he'd texted her. He hadn't.

She sighed heavily, mentally preparing herself to hear the words *I didn't get the part* and running through all the different ways she could console Drake. Then she asked Lori to have her car brought up and headed out the door.

Chapter Two

"Sasha, please, calm down," Amanda said.

The friends were wrapping up their lunch, and while Sasha had drained three glasses of Bellinis, she'd barely touched her salad. She just didn't have an appetite.

"Had Drake's audition gone badly," Amanda continued, "he would've called hours ago. I bet it's going so great that he hasn't been able to break away and contact you."

Sasha closed her eyes and massaged her temples, wishing she'd never arranged the audition in the first place. "I don't know. I just have a bad feeling about this. I bet Drake bombed the audition and he's too embarrassed to tell me."

"I *absolutely* don't think that's the case," Amanda argued, paying the bill before they got up and headed downstairs. When her car arrived, she turned to Sasha. "I'm sorry, girl-friend, but I'm still hopeful. I really do think you're going to get good news."

"From your lips to Gary Rosen's ears," Sasha replied, struggling to crack a smile. "Thank you for lunch."

"Anytime. I have to stop by Lady Faye's radio interview with Power Ninety-Nine before I head back to the office, so I'll see you later this afternoon. Fingers crossed you'll hear something soon."

Sasha raised her hand and crossed her fingers. "Let's hope so."

As soon as Amanda drove off, the valet brought Sasha's car around. She climbed inside, threw her purse in the passenger seat, and resisted the urge to scream. She checked her cell once again. Still no message or missed call from Drake. And then, just as she locked the phone and put her car in drive, a text message popped up. It was him.

Sasha jerked the phone up towards her face so fast that she almost knocked herself out. Her hands were trembling to the point that it took three attempts to type in the security code before she got it right. After what seemed like forever, she was finally able to open Drake's text message.

Hey, babe. Sorry I didn't reach out sooner, but I'm just now leaving the audition. That place was a madhouse. Are you busy, or can you meet me at my place?

"Are you kidding me?" Sasha yelled. She typed frantically.

Yes, I can meet you, but I'm dying to know how things went. Can you talk?

Drake wrote back.

I'll see you at my place . . .

"Oh, I'm going to kill you, making me wait like this." Sasha screeched away from the curb and tore down the street, hoping that traffic wouldn't be too crazy on the way to his downtown loft.

She quickly bobbed and weaved through traffic, arriving at Drake's door in record time. Sasha knocked lightly, then opened it with the set of keys he'd given her a couple of months earlier.

When she walked inside, Sasha was greeted by darkness. The blinds were in blackout mode, and candles were lit along the floor, creating a pathway leading straight to the bedroom.

She furrowed her brows in confusion. "Drake?"

"In the bedroom, babe. Come join me . . ."

"What is this man up to now?" she murmured.

Sasha walked back to the bedroom, and there was Drake, lying naked across his king-size bed and holding two champagne glasses. A huge smile was spread across his face.

"What in the world is going on?" she asked. "I've been on pins and needles all day waiting to hear from you. Do you have any idea what I've been going—"

"Sasha, my love, please," Drake interrupted. "Calm down, take off your clothes, and come join me. Once you do that, I'll tell you everything."

Sasha closed her eyes and exhaled, dropping her shoulders and allowing her body to relax. She stepped out of her dress and shoes. Before she could unhook her bra and slip off her thong, Drake set the glasses on the nightstand, slid off the bed, and removed them for her.

"So does this mean you've got good news?" she asked.

He remained silent, pressing his warm body against hers while slowly wrapping his arms around her waist. Drake kissed her deeply, his hands grasping her back.

Sasha responded by running her fingers through his hair, kissing him with the same passionate energy until he tore himself away and grabbed the champagne glasses.

"Drumroll, please." He beamed, handing one to her. "You're looking at Cliff Bailey, leading man in Gary Rosen's *On Bended Knee.* I got the part!"

Sasha screamed and jumped up and down so frantically she spilled champagne all over her breasts.

Drake immediately bent down and lapped it up while sucking and caressing her hardened nipples.

"Sweetie," Sasha choked, struggling to hold back tears while holding him tightly, "I am so proud of you. I've been worried all day. That is such wonderful music to my ears.

Do you understand what this means for your career? I mean, seriously. This is it! This is the one. You're about to be Hollywood gold. You'll be able to walk into any room and get any part you want. A Gary Rosen film means A-plus-*plus* list status."

"I know. I know! I couldn't be happier. I also wouldn't have been able to do it without you." Drake grabbed the champagne bottle and refilled Sasha's glass. "Let's try this again." He chuckled. "A toast. To the best publicist in the business. I thank you. You've turned my career around and taken it straight to the top. I am forever grateful."

"Aw, thank you. It only goes up from here." Sasha clinked her glass against Drake's. "To us, our continued success, and our unlimited futures."

"Hear, hear!"

Drake and Sasha took a sip of champagne, then set their glasses down on the nightstand. He took her hand in his and led her towards the bed, laying her down while her legs hung over the side. Then he got down on his knees, spread her thighs apart, and buried his face deep between them.

Sasha moaned seductively and arched her back, grabbing Drake's head and pushing it even closer towards her. His tongue quickly flickered over her clit, then slid down and glided around her entrance. Just when her muscles quivered uncontrollably, he rolled his tongue over her clit again. He teased her throbbing flesh lightly with his teeth while plunging his fingers inside her. She quickly came.

Sasha's body was still trembling while Drake climbed onto the bed and kneeled over her, positioning his cock above her face. She parted her lips and allowed him to enter, gripping the base while tightening her jaws around the shaft. She reached between Drake's legs and grabbed his ass, pushing him farther in. As he plunged deeper, she held her breath, the head of his dick tickling the back of her throat.

Drake grunted loudly. His body shook. He pulled away quickly, moving between her legs and thrusting his cock inside her. Sasha wrapped her hands around his neck while gyrating her pelvis in rhythm with his. He bent down and lightly bit her lips while she stared into his eyes, smiling deviously.

"Fuck me, Cliff Bailey," she whispered. "Fuck me *good*."

"Oh, is that what we're doing now?" Drake panted. "Role playing?"

"Why, yes, Mr. Bailey, I believe we are."

"Well, in that case . . ."

Drake's strokes suddenly grew stronger, faster, and more passionate. Sasha dug her fingernails into his back and screamed out his name. She bit into his shoulder, and together their bodies shuddered in unison.

A spent Drake fell onto the other side of the bed.

Sasha turned over and snuggled up against him. "You know I'm supposed to be back at the office."

"You just helped your biggest client land the role of a lifetime. I don't think Nick will mind if you take the afternoon off."

"You're right. He's gonna be thrilled when I tell him the news." Sasha climbed out of bed and pulled her phone from her tote. She checked her voicemail, then scrolled through her email. "It looks like the coast is clear. No emergencies or fires that need to be put out immediately. So I can play hooky and spend the rest of the day with you."

"Yay!" Drake cheered.

"But"—Sasha laughed—"I do need to text Nick and Amanda and let them know you got the part. They've both been frantically waiting to hear the news."

While Sasha stood next to the bed composing her texts, Drake walked over and kneeled in front of her. He spread her legs apart and flicked his tongue over her clit furiously.

She became unsteady on her feet and held on to Drake's shoulder with one hand while attempting to type with the other.

"So you can't even let me send these messages before jumping off to round two?"

"Hell no," Drake replied. "Not with your fine ass standing over me naked. Now hurry up so I can give you another dose of this dick."

"You are something else." Sasha giggled, struggling to get through her texts while Drake slid his tongue deeper between her legs.

The minute she hit the *send* button, he sat on the bed, and Sasha climbed on top of him, her thighs straddling his hips.

"Ride it and show Daddy how proud you are of him," he insisted, grabbing her ass and shoving his erection inside her.

"Oh, I'm gonna ride it all right," Sasha responded seductively, throwing her arms over his shoulders and grinding her pelvis in slow circles.

"You feel so good, baby. You're going to give it to me all day, every day, until I have to leave for this shoot. That's the only way I'll be able to make it."

"I will. Don't you worry."

Later that evening, Sasha and Drake officially celebrated his new role over steak and lobster at Garcelle's Prime House. They were joined by Drake's agent, Damon, and his partner, Cameron, along with Nick and his wife Chloe.

While it had been a wonderful evening filled with laughter and well-wishes, Sasha couldn't help but feel a little down over the fact that Drake was leaving town to begin filming the following week. She'd had no idea shooting would start so soon. She'd been discreetly checking her calendar throughout the evening to see when she could fly to

New York to visit Drake on set.

"Ladies and gentlemen," Nick said. "Thank you for a fantastic evening. Drake, congratulations again. You make Kline and Associates look so good. And Sasha, thank you as well. Without you, we're nothing."

"I could say the same for you all as well." Sasha smiled. "But thank you, that's very kind of you to say."

"Yes, it is," Drake chimed in. "I appreciate you all."

"Cheers," Damon said, holding his glass in the air for one last toast. "To a successful shoot and an awesome, profitable movie."

The group clinked their glasses together before draining them and getting up to leave. Everyone said their goodbyes and retrieved their cars from the valet, then went their separate ways.

Sasha was quiet when Drake drove back to her house.

"What's the matter, babe?" he asked.

She turned and stared out the window, blinking rapidly in an effort to hold back the tears threatening to fall. "I'm not ready for you to leave. And I didn't realize how emotional I'd be once things got real. I thought we'd have more time together before filming began."

Drake reached over and grabbed Sasha's hand. "So did I. But we'll work it out. You can come to New York and see me whenever your schedule permits, and I'll get back to LA when I can."

Sasha looked over at Drake and smiled.

He kissed her hand, then caressed it softy with his tongue.

The ticklish sensation sent a thrill straight through her. She squirmed and checked the navigation system to see how much longer it would take to get back to her house.

Drake eyed her lustfully. "Should I step on it?" he asked, speeding up as soon as he'd asked the question.

"Yes, you should," she replied, slipping her hand in his

lap and gently squeezing his erection.

Drake hit the accelerator, keeping one hand on the steering wheel while gliding the other underneath her skirt.

"You'd better hurry up and get us home before I make you stop this car so I can have my way with you." Sasha sighed. She opened her legs wider while he stroked her clit, continuing to massage his dick fervently.

"Don't tempt me," he groaned, making a sharp turn onto Wilshire Boulevard and tearing down the street.

Drake swerved into the driveway, and he and Sasha stumbled up the walkway, unable to keep their hands off of each other. He unlocked the door, and they tumbled inside. She kicked the door closed, and they tore one another's clothes off. Drake grabbed Sasha's waist and led her into the living room, where she fell onto the couch and pulled him on top of her.

Their hands, lips, and tongues intertwined. Within minutes Drake was deep inside Sasha, thrusting wildly as she grinded to the pace of each stroke. The innate passion between them was undeniable, and Sasha was determined make every moment together count until it was time for Drake to leave.

Chapter Three

*K*eep *it together. Keep it together. Keep it together.*
Sasha was sitting in Kline & Associates' conference room, struggling not to fall apart during the middle of their staff meeting. Drake had left for New York that morning, and she couldn't believe how devastated she was over his departure.

Sasha and Amanda had gone out for coffee that morning, and as Sasha sulked over her iced macchiato, Amanda reminded her that this was the first time she and Drake had actually been apart. Since they'd begun dating, all of his movie shoots had taken place in either Los Angeles or a nearby city. He was always just a car ride away. But now she couldn't just hop up and go see him whenever she wanted. This time they were almost twenty-five hundred miles apart, so her anguish was understandable.

What was worse were the demands of their jobs. Drake's hectic filming schedule took up practically all of his time and energy. The same went for Sasha and her jam-packed roster of high-maintenance clients. Between the two of them, she couldn't see when they'd be able to get away and spend time together.

But one thing they did have to look forward to was their trip to Cabo. Planning that vacation had been a nice reprieve for Sasha. She was so looking forward to the time off, when Drake would be done filming and she'd be in between press events. She had narrowed their resort choices down to two, chosen a few sets of dates, and created a list of potential activities. Now all she had to do was compose a fun Valentine's-Day-themed group email containing all the pertinent information and send it to their parents. However, that small component was causing Sasha the most anxiety.

Her goal was to create an unforgettable experience that everyone would enjoy. But considering Drake's parents were the polar opposite of hers, she just didn't know whether it would be possible to appease everyone. While her parents still lived in the working-class neighborhood she'd grown up in on Chicago's south side, Drake's parents resided in a sprawling home in Greenwich, Connecticut. Her parents' idea of a fun night out involved playing bingo in their church's basement after having a soul food buffet dinner at Ruthie's Kitchen. Drake's parents, on the other hand, enjoyed attending operas and ballets and dining on raw vegan cuisine at their country club. So needless to say, arranging a trip that would please the entire group was going to be quite the challenge.

"Okay, gang, that's all I've got," Nick said, his booming voice snapping Sasha out of her thoughts. He turned to her and raised his eyebrows. "You've been uncharacteristically quiet. Anything you'd like to add?"

"No, actually," she replied. She'd purposely remained silent throughout the meeting in an effort to speed things up so she could get back to her office and continue working on her vacation email. "I think Lori did a great job of including everything I'm currently managing in the agenda, so I'm all set."

"All right then," Nick said, picking up his notebook. "Thanks, everyone. Have a great week."

Sasha hurried out of the conference room and back to her office. But the minute she sat at her desk, Nick appeared in the doorway.

"Hey, one thing I forgot to mention during the meeting.

Mitch Morrison. Does that name ring a bell?"

"It does," Sasha responded, hoping this conversation wasn't going in the direction she suspected it was. "What about him?"

"His agent called me today, and he's looking for a new publicist. The guy's got a huge future ahead of him. His last movie *Far Beyond* grossed over one hundred million dollars at the box office, and he is in high demand. He's young, good-looking, extremely likeable, and has that *wow* factor. Everyone thinks he's going to be the next Will Smith. So, I was thinking . . ."

When his voice trailed off, Sasha chimed in. "So you want me to sign him," she said, eyeing holiday templates on her computer before turning her attention to Nick. "Well, I'll say this. Mitch is definitely talented and has mass appeal. I do think he's got the potential to go far. I also think we'd work well together, in that we have a lot in common."

"I couldn't agree more," Nick said. "You two are fairly close in age, you grew up not too far from one another. with you being from Chicago and him from Rockford, Illinois."

"Plus we're both African-American and working hard to compete in this tough, oftentimes discriminatory business while proving the worth of our voice."

"Exactly! So it's a done deal then," Nick bellowed.

"Not so fast," Sasha interjected. "At this point, Mitch's résumé is still a bit too thin for me to take him on right now, especially considering how swamped I am. On top of my standing obligations with my usual suspects, I've got a ton of promotional events planned here in the States as well as overseas for Drake's movie *On Bended Knee*. The last thing I'd want to do is overextend myself by signing Mitch without being able to provide him with the undivided attention he'd need in order to elevate his career."

"So I take it that's a no?"

"Take it as a not right now."

"Got it." Nick sighed. "I respect your decision, but I think you should reconsider. You two would make such a great team. I could assign him to someone else, but I'm going to hold off. I have a feeling you're gonna change your mind."

"We'll see . . ."

Nick tapped Sasha's doorframe in defeat. "Alrighty, then. Let me know if you decide otherwise."

"Will do."

And with that, Sasha turned back to her computer, selected a heart-shaped template, and began filling in the trip details.

Sasha rolled her overstuffed suitcase towards the door, then ran back into the bedroom to grab her phone charger. Just when she thought she had everything and could finally head out to her awaiting car, she realized she'd left her laptop in the kitchen.

"Girl," she said to herself, rushing through the living room and grabbing the computer off the countertop. She was so beside herself that she couldn't seem to think straight. It had been almost three weeks since she'd seen Drake, and she was finally heading to New York to spend some time with him.

The pair had managed to call, text, email, and video chat throughout the days, but it wasn't the same as being together in person. Sasha believed in the phrase *absence makes the heart grow fonder* more than ever now, because Drake being gone had somehow made her love him even more.

She slid her laptop inside her tote and headed outside. The driver, who was waiting on the other side of the door, took her suitcase and led her to the car.

"Good morning, Miss Williams."

"Good morning, Teddy."

"I've checked the route to the airport, and traffic is pretty clear, so you should arrive at LAX sooner than expected."

"Awesome, thank you," Sasha replied giddily.

Teddy opened her door, and she climbed inside, resisting the urge to wiggle in her seat. She'd been anticipating this moment since the day she'd dropped Drake off at the airport, and now that it was finally here, she was finding it hard to suppress her joy.

Sasha and Teddy made small talk as he drove down the Interstate 405 freeway. When they reached Sepulveda Boulevard, she stared out the window, and her stomach flipped. They were getting close to the airport. She glanced down at her watch. Her flight wasn't due to depart for another two hours. That would give her plenty of time to check her bag, go through security, get a coffee, and browse the new releases at her favorite bookstore.

When Teddy turned onto LAX's World Way, her phone buzzed. She couldn't help but giggle, already knowing it was Drake calling to ask whether she'd made it to the airport. Sasha grabbed her phone and looked down at the screen. Drake had actually sent her a text, and oddly enough, so had about fifty other people. She scrolled through her notifications and saw messages from Nick, Amanda, Lori, several other coworkers, and many of her media associates.

Oh shit. This can't be good . . . .

Sasha opened Drake's message first, her eyes widening and then tearing up as she read.

Hey, babe. Can't talk right now, but I've got bad news. Gary and I got into a huge fight on set, and I got fired. I apologized profusely and tried to smooth things over, but it's a done deal. This asshole already replaced me, too. I'm so sorry. I know how hard you worked to get me on this project. I'll explain everything when I get home. I'm at LaGuardia Airport now. See you soon. Love you.

Sasha's mouth fell open. Her heart seemed to be thumping out of her chest. Waves of angry heat washed over her. She was in utter shock, so much that she didn't even realize Teddy had already parked the car and opened her door.

"Miss Williams? Are you okay?"

"No," she choked, unable to hold back the tears that had trickled down her cheek. "The trip is off. I'm sorry. Could you please take me back home?"

"Of course," he replied quickly, closing her door and placing her suitcase in the trunk.

As Teddy hurried back inside the car and pulled off, Sasha texted Lori and asked her to cancel her flights and hotel. She could barely see the keys on her phone through the angry mist in her eyes. She struggled to steady her breathing. Now she knew why everyone was texting her. A quick *Google* search showed that *TMZ* had reported the news of Drake being fired thirty minutes ago. Sasha clicked on the link.

BREAKING NEWS: Hot-headed bad-boy actor Drake Lancaster strikes again! According to on-set sources, Drake was just fired from legendary director Gary Rosen's highly anticipated Valentine's Day rom-com, On Bended Knee.

"It was brutal," a source who asked to remain anonymous revealed. "Drake just lost it after Gary cut a scene and changed a few of his lines. The minute Drake raised his voice and flailed his arms in protest, security was called, and Gary had him removed from the set."

Another anonymous source went on to reveal that Gary was hesitant to hire Drake in the first place and now regrets his decision. "Gary wishes he'd stuck to his guns and never even considered Drake for this film. But everyone assured him that Drake had changed. Clearly, he hasn't. And I'm no psychic, but I think it's safe to say Drake just killed his career."

Word on the street is that talented up-and-comer Mitch Morri-son has already been tapped as Drake's replacement. Story developing . . .

Sasha felt sick to her stomach. She pulled a tissue from her tote and dabbed tears from her cheeks. As much as she didn't want to believe anything she'd just read, it sounded quite realistic. Gary was known for being a perfectionist and constantly tweaking dialogue during filming. Drake liked to study his scripts well in advance and stick to exactly what he'd memorized while shooting. But with a prominent direc-tor like Gary, Sasha couldn't believe Drake hadn't compro-mised. *On Bended Knee* was the opportunity of a lifetime, so losing his cool over a change in lines was inexcusable. And while Sasha was great at her job, she couldn't help but won-der how the hell she'd get him out of this mess.

Sasha's phone was vibrating nonstop with calls, emails, and texts. She ignored them all and scrolled down to Nick's message.

I'm sure you've already heard the news that Drake's been fired from On Bended Knee. *Mitch Morrison has been confirmed as his replacement. Unfortunate for Drake, but I think you should reconsider signing Mitch. It's groundbreaking that an African-American actor is taking on a lead role that was originally written for a white male, amongst an all-star, predominately white cast, in a Gary Rosen film, no less. Trust me, Mitch is the real deal, the next big thing. Doesn't all that warrant a change of heart?*

Sasha pondered Nick's message. She knew he was right. This was a prime opportunity for both her and Mitch. As for Drake, he'd made his own bed. That didn't mean she had to lie in it with him.

She took a deep breath and hit the *reply* button.

Yes, it does. I'll be in this afternoon to draw up Mitch's paperwork, since my trip to NY was suddenly cancelled.

Nick responded immediately.

Sorry, Sash. I know this is a tough call, but business is business. You're doing the right thing. See you soon.

She tossed her phone back in her tote and stared out the window, exhaling while willing her anger to subside. She was still shocked that Drake had managed to get fired from the biggest role of his career. She was also irritated that he'd probably be upset over her signing Mitch. But as the saying went, the show must go on. Just as Drake had made the choice to lose his cool and jeopardize his career, she'd made the choice to rep a great actor and further enhance hers.

"I'm so fucking pissed!" Drake yelled, pacing Sasha's living room floor while holding his head in his hands. "I mean . . . seriously. I didn't even get that loud with the dude. All I asked was that he reconsider keeping two of the lines that he wanted to remove. Two! Then the next thing you know, I'm being escorted off the set by security . . ."

As Drake continued to rant, Sasha sat on couch, rubbing her temples and watching him stomp back and forth. He was too angry to be challenged, so for the time being she decided to keep quiet and let him get it all out.

"My dressing room hadn't even been cleared out before Mitch Morrison was brought on to replace me. *Mitch Morrison.* I mean, does anybody even know who the hell he is? He's been in a couple of movies or whatever, but his portfolio can't compete with mine. And I bet you *On Bended Knee* is gonna completely flop now that I've been replaced with a nobody."

Sasha stirred in her seat, knowing that now was not the

time to mention she'd signed Mitch earlier that afternoon.

Drake turned to her with his arms out at his sides. "Don't you have anything to say about all this? Have you reached out to your media contacts to clear my name yet?"

"Babe, please, calm down. Yes, I released a statement to the press hours ago, which I already emailed to you. I'm doing the best I can to put out this fire, but I'm not gonna lie. This is a really bad look. Gary's name is pristine in the business, so unfortunately, everyone is probably going to side with him. However, I've made a huge push to present the entire incident as one big misunderstanding."

"Okay . . . okay," Drake said, a glimmer of hope in his eyes. He ran his fingers through his hair and paced the floor again. "And in the meantime, I'll have you and Damon make some calls and set up meetings with producers and directors. I'm sure there's another big-screen Valentine's Day movie in the works that would want me as the lead."

A sharp pang hit her in the chest. She stood and walked over to Drake, gently placing her hand on his shoulder. "Sweetie, Damon and I have been on the phone all day with practically everyone we know in the industry. Neither of us were able to secure a meeting for you. It's just too soon after the altercation."

Drake froze, then took a step back and gripped the edge of the bar. His mouth fell open, but nothing came out. Then finally, he spoke up. "So nobody's willing to see me? Not one person?"

"Unfortunately, no. Not right now. But give it some time, babe. Let things blow over. Meanwhile, I've put together an awesome community service schedule for you and sent an accompanying press release out to the media. Hopefully all the journalists and bloggers will report on your good deeds, which would help clear your name."

Drake turned away from her. "I can't believe this is actually happening. One minute I'm the hottest actor in town, standing in the middle of Manhattan shooting the biggest movie of my career. Then the next minute, I'm kicked off the film and being blackballed by the entire industry."

"For now," Sasha chimed in. "But we've got a great plan in place. So just stick to it, lay low, and we'll get you back up and running in no time." *Or so I hope . . .*

Drake nodded, his red eyes puffy, his expression filled with dread.

"Can I make you a hot cup of tea or something to eat?" she asked softly.

"No, thanks. I don't have an appetite. I really just wanna lie down."

Sasha tilted her head and gave Drake a sly smile. "Would you like for me to join you?" she offered, hoping that one of their hot, steamy lovemaking sessions would help lift his spirits. But instead of saying yes, he grabbed his things and headed towards the door.

"Actually, I think I need to be by myself right now. I've gotta wrap my head around all this and figure out my next move."

"Oh . . . all right. Well, I'm here for you. Let me know if you need anything."

"Thanks. I'll call you later."

Sasha slumped her shoulders as she stood in the doorway and watched Drake walk to his car, his head hanging low. She wished there was more she could do to help him. Better yet, she wished he'd never gotten himself in this predicament in the first place. "Why must you be so hot-headed?" She dreaded the uphill battle they were about to face.

Her phone pinged, pulling her away from the door. She checked it. A message from Mitch.

Hey, boss! Just had to send you a quick shout-out and once again thank you for signing me. So honored to have you on the team. I'm already on set in NY and killed my first two scenes. Gary's been great, and the cast and crew welcomed me with open arms. It's all happening so fast, but I'm beyond grateful. Would love to do a quick video chat with you sometime tomorrow so we can officially meet — if you can call that official lol. Then next time I'm in town we'll definitely connect in person. Let me know if your schedule permits. Forever appreciative, M.M.

Mitch's message put a huge smile on Sasha's face. His excitement and gratitude were a breath of fresh air after dealing with the fallout of Drake's incident. She hit the *reply* button and typed her response.

Congratulations on landing the role, and I'm glad to be a part of the team. Looking forward to what will surely be a prosperous partnership. Happy to hear things are going well on set. I'm free tomorrow any time after four in the afternoon PST, so feel free to reach out when you can. Chat soon! S.M.

After Sasha sent the message, she resisted the urge to call Drake and check on him. He'd made it clear he wanted to be alone, so she chose to respect that.

She pulled up her email, hoping her parents and the Lancasters had sent back their vacation preferences. When she saw they hadn't, Sasha opened the internet and performed a search on Mitch in hopes of finding out everything there was to know about him before their video chat.

Chapter Four

Sasha was sitting behind her desk at work sipping on her third iced macchiato. Her nerves were in complete shambles. She had just gotten off the phone with Drake's agent, and neither of them had good news to share. As hard as they both were trying, neither of them could get Drake in front of anyone in the industry. His confrontation with Gary had virtually relegated him beyond the Z-list. They couldn't even book him an audition for an indie film or an off-off-Broadway play. Sasha had figured things would be bad, but she'd never dreamed they'd be *this* bad.

On top of that, the planning of the Cabo trip had gone from challenging to damn near impossible. Drake's parents insisted they were only available during one of the suggested weekends while Sasha's parents insisted on the other. The Lancasters wanted to stay at the Villa del Sueño, while the Williams requested the Casa del Fiesta. And the Lancasters chose whale watching, jet skiing, and swimming with the dolphins as their main activities, while the Williams selected a camel safari, taco and tequila night, and salsa dance lessons as theirs.

This is going to be a fucking disaster. Her thoughts were interrupted when a video chat request popped up on her computer. It was Mitch.

Sasha grabbed her compact and checked her hair and makeup, then accepted the request.

"Hello, Mitch," she said, trying not to appear as surprised as she felt when his image appeared. For some reason, he looked even more handsome on her screen than he did in his movies and photos. A younger Omari Hardwick came to mind when Sasha studied his dark emotive eyes, smooth mocha complexion, and the shadow of a beard covering his chiseled jawline. "How are you?

"I'm great! How are you?"

"I could be unprofessional and say terrible, but I won't." She laughed. "I'm doing well."

"No, no, please." Mitch chuckled, licking his full, shapely lips then revealing a perfectly straight-toothed smile. "You can keep it one hundred with me. If you're having a bad day, then that's what it is. I don't ever want you to feel as though you can't share something like that with me."

"Well, thank you." Sasha grinned, forcing herself to stop swiveling in her chair. "I may take you up on that offer one of these days, but not today. We've got a lot to cover, starting with all the press events you'll be attending for *On Bended Knee* throughout the States and overseas. So hold on tight, because you're about to take quite a ride. This is the big time. Are you ready for it?"

"I stay ready so I won't have to get ready," Mitch shot back, flashing that five-star smile again. "I'm just glad to have you by my side, taking the ride with me."

Sasha emitted an uncontrollable schoolgirl giggle. *Girl, please pull yourself together . . .*

"And now," Mitch continued, "if I may have a moment of unprofessionalism, Sasha, you are absolutely stunning. I mean, I've seen photos of you and all, but *damn*. I didn't realize you were this fine."

Sasha inhaled sharply and froze, not quite knowing how to respond. Luckily, she didn't have to once Mitch steered the conversation back in the right direction.

"Okay, I'm done," he declared. "I said it. Now, back to business."

"Yes, back to business," she echoed, glad her brown skin wouldn't reveal the blushing red heat nipping at her cheeks. "So for starters, I've put together an *On Bended Knee* tentative press schedule that's already been approved by the producers. I'll email that to you this afternoon, and once you've approved it, I'll forward it on to the media outlets. I've also created an extensive list of publications, radio shows, podcasts, blogs, and so forth that I'd like you to interview with over the course of the next several months. We'll work together to schedule those as your calendar permits. Then I've got a few photo shoots planned, and a consultant who's going to work with you to update your portfolio. Once we knock those things out, we'll move on to the next steps that'll further boost your career. Sound good so far?"

"Sounds phenomenal so far," Mitch replied, giving Sasha a round of applause. "You know, I've always heard great things about you, but within the first five minutes of this conversation, I'm completely blown away. How did you manage to impress me so quickly, especially considering how hard I am to please?"

"Hey, what can I say?" Sasha joked, patting herself on the back. "But no, seriously, I've been in the game for a long time, and I know what it takes to elevate careers. Unfortunately for us, and you know what I mean by *us*, we have to work that much harder in order to get ours. You feel me?"

"I absolutely feel you, sis. That's why I'm so ecstatic to have you on my team. You know the struggle. But you also know what it takes to help me shatter that glass ceiling and rise above it."

"I most certainly do," Sasha said right before a knock sounded at Mitch's door.

"Come in!" he called out.

A production assistant stuck his head inside. "Mister Morrison? Mister Rosen is ready for you."

"Tell him I'll be right there," Mitch replied, never once taking his gaze off Sasha.

"So I'll email you the materials that correspond with everything we just went over, and you can let me know if you have any questions," she told him.

"Perfect. I'm glad we did this. It's funny, after this brief video chat I feel like I've known you for years. You've got great energy, Sasha. I'm looking forward to talking with you more. And we definitely have to link up next time I'm in LA."

"Absolutely. Just let me know when you're in town. Meanwhile, you'd better get to the set. You already know Gary ain't no joke."

"You think I don't, when I do? I'm on it. I'm not giving that A-plus-*plus* director nooo problems."

"Please don't." Sasha laughed.

"It was great chatting with you. I'll hit you up soon. Thanks for everything."

"You're welcome, Mitch. Thank you, as well. Talk to you soon."

Sasha disconnected the chat, then stared off into space, completely dumbfounded. In that moment, she couldn't quite comprehend how she felt. But one thing she did know was that the exhilarating feeling swirling around in her chest was nothing that a woman in a committed relationship should be experiencing.

Her thoughts were interrupted by the buzzing of her phone. It was a text message from Mitch. Sasha's stomach performed an involuntary backflip.

Thank you again for that amazing introduction. Can't wait to meet you in person and see what magic you and I can create together. Until then . . . M.M.

"Oh my damn," Sasha whispered, stealing one of her

grandmother's infamous phrases.

Just as she began typing a response, a text from Drake popped up. She opened it immediately while trying not to feel guilty over her exchange with Mitch.

Hey, I'm still in bed. In no mood to get up and read more nega-tive stories about myself. You got any good news? Were you or Damon able to book anything for me? And what's going on with the Cabo trip? Have you picked a departure date and booked the resort and scheduled the activities? I really want my parents to have a good time, so I hope you're on top of things. Let me know. And what's for dinner?

Sasha was so irritated she wanted to throw her phone across the room. She resisted the urge to hit the *reply* button and curse Drake out, and instead closed his message, reo-pened Mitch's, and typed a response.

I'm looking forward to meeting you in person as well. I antici-pate a great working relationship between us and an extremely bright future for you. Let's get that sit-down in LA on the calendar soon. Take care, and happy shooting! S.W.

Sasha decided to call Amanda and ask whether she was available for dinner, which she was. After sending Drake a text letting him know he'd be on his own tonight, she called and reserved a table at The Polo Lounge. Then she turned back to her computer. Rather than contact her parents and the Lancasters in an effort to sort out their vacation plans, Sasha pulled up *Google Images* and scrolled through Mitch's red-carpet photos to see who he'd been hanging out with, then did a little research on his dating history.

Sasha stood in front of the bathroom mirror, swiping shim-mery gloss over her lips. She was wearing a black suede minidress and python stilettos. Loose curls cascaded down her back, and delicate silver jewelry hung from her ears and neck.

Her cell phone buzzed. It was a text message, asking whether she'd be at the Platinum Hotel's Diamond VIP Bar at eight o'clock. She replied *yes*, then gave herself one last look in the mirror before heading into the living room.

Drake was sprawled out on her couch, eating chips and drinking beer while watching television. He wasn't wearing a shirt, and his belly protruded over his sweatpants. It was a sight she'd never seen until now. But considering he'd been eating nonstop and hadn't been to the gym in weeks, she wasn't surprised.

"Damn, babe," he said before expelling a loud belch. "Where're you going dressed like that?"

"Out for drinks with Amanda," Sasha replied, wrinkling her nose in disgust.

"Cool. Tell her I said hello." Drake picked up his phone and began typing furiously.

"What are you up to tonight?" Sasha asked, hoping he'd come up with a productive response.

"Chillin'. Watching football. I just ordered a pizza and wings, so don't worry about cooking or picking anything up for me. I've got it covered."

Sasha watched in disbelief as Drake stuck his hand down his pants. What a difference a matter of weeks had made. He'd gone from being a working, go-getting, A-list actor to a depressed, unmotivated couch potato. Aside from all the encouragement she'd been giving him mentally and emotionally, Sasha tried persuading Drake to reach out to his actor friends for support, or getting a stress-relieving workout in, but he'd refused. All he wanted to do was lie around, feel sorry for himself, and wait for her and Damon to perform a career-restoring miracle.

"I'm leaving," Sasha said, grabbing her clutch and heading towards the door. "I won't be out too late. Enjoy your dinner and the game."

"See ya."

The minute Sasha was out of the house, her spirits lifted. It felt good to get away and spend time with people whose energy matched hers. She'd actually been looking forward to tonight all week.

When she arrived at the hotel, Sasha left her car with the valet and headed to the top floor. All eyes were on her as she greeted the hostess then walked through the dark, chic bar. She approached the private section located in the back, where a bouncer unhooked a velvet rope and led her to a corner booth.

"Here you are, Miss Williams. Your guest went to the restroom but will be back shortly. And that's a bottle of our best champagne waiting for you on the table."

"Wonderful, thank you."

Sasha slid inside the booth and took a deep breath. She turned around to see if she knew anyone there, then heard a familiar voice greet her from behind.

"Hello, beautiful."

She turned back around and laid eyes on Mitch.

"It's so good to finally see you in the flesh," he continued. "Thank you for meeting me."

Being in front of Mitch practically took her breath away. He'd somehow managed to appear even more handsome in person.

"Hello. It's good to see you, too."

Sasha stood, and she and Mitch shared a warm embrace that lasted much longer than necessary.

"Please, have a seat," he said, pouring two glasses of champagne and handing one to her. "Before we get started,

let's have a toast. To our partnership. May it be both ful-
filling and satisfying for us both. Cheers."

"Cheers," Sasha said, clinking her glass against Mitch's
then taking a sip of champagne. "Mmm, this is delicious."

"I ordered the best. Just for you."

"Thank you," Sasha said softly, willing herself not to feel
any sort of attraction towards this man.

After a few more sips of champagne and a bit of small
talk, the nervous ball of energy still stuck in her chest slowly
unraveled. The lightweight banter eventually turned into a
deeper conversation, and she learned that there was much
more to Mitch than just his handsome face and muscular
physique. He, too, had grown up in a working-class family,
and while neither of his parents had attended college, they'd
insisted that both Mitch and his younger brother do so.
Mitch had studied theater at Northwestern University, while
his brother pursued an engineering degree at the University
of Illinois.

"But my parents weren't just about education," Mitch
said. "They didn't play about religion or community service
work. To this day I still attend church every Sunday, and I
created an organization that funds special needs programs in
Los Angeles's public schools."

"Wow, that is amazing, Mitch. How admirable."

As the conversation continued, Sasha and Mitch realized
they had several friends in common back home. And even
though they agreed that they both loved LA due to the beau-
ty, weather, and it being the entertainment capital of the
world, they both missed the seasons, the deep-dish pizza,
and stunning downtown skyline that Chicago boasted.

Mitch shared with Sasha that he was single, but she ne-
glected to mention Drake, figuring Mitch probably already
knew about their relationship since they'd gone public last
year. He talked about LA's crazy dating scene and shared

that he'd love to one day get married and have children, but as of right now, he was fine just focusing on his career.

By the end of the evening, Sasha felt as though she had known Mitch for years. And she'd enjoyed herself so much she didn't feel guilty for lying to Drake about being with Amanda. But she did wonder how in the hell she was going to break the news to him that she'd signed Mitch. *Cross that bridge when you get to it.*

"This was really great, Sasha. I'm so glad we finally got together. But I should probably head out. I've got a super early flight back to New York in the morning."

"And the last thing we want is for you to miss it," Sasha quipped as she and Mitch exited the bar. "I'm really glad we did this, too. I couldn't be happier having you on board, and I can't wait to watch your career skyrocket."

"With you by my side, there's nothing I can't accomplish."

When Sasha and Mitch walked outside, her car was already waiting.

"That's me right there." She pointed, handing her ticket to the valet.

Mitch led her to the car and opened the door. "We should do this again next time I'm in town."

"I'd like that."

"Cool. And the scenes I'm shooting for *On Bended Knee* are actually wrapping way earlier than expected, so I may be back home sooner than I thought. That would be nice, wouldn't it?"

"It would be . . ." Sasha felt herself melting at the sound of Mitch's deep voice and the sight of his inviting smile.

He wrapped his arms around her waist and pulled her close. She placed her hands on his shoulders, inhaling the scent of his woodsy cologne. He gazed into her eyes, as if he were searching for what she wanted next. Then he took her face in his hands and leaned in. Just when his lips almost touched hers, she turned her head, and the kiss landed on her cheek instead.

"I'd better go," Sasha said, turning around and climbing inside her car. "Thanks again for tonight."

"No, thank *you*. Text me when you get home so that I'll know you made it safely."

"I will."

Sasha watched while Mitch sauntered towards an awaiting town car. The driver jumped out and opened the door. Right before he got in, Mitch turned around and blew Sasha a kiss. She couldn't help but smile and gave him a slight wave. Then she drove off, feeling as though she were floating on air.

But once she hit the freeway and reality set in, Sasha began to panic. *What in the hell are you doing*? But she knew exactly what she was doing—falling.

When Sasha arrived home, she walked into the living room. Drake was still lying on the couch, now in a deep sleep. A pizza box was on the coffee table, along with a container filled with chicken bones, drained beer bottles, and a huge empty potato chip bag.

Sasha groaned, kicking off her shoes and quietly cleaning up. Once she was done, she contemplated waking Drake so he could come to bed. But after standing there watching him snore loudly, she decided against it and headed to the bedroom.

Sasha pulled off her dress and wrapped her hair in a silk scarf, then sent Mitch a text letting him know she was home. He replied immediately.

Good, glad you made it in safely. Oh, and btw, I think I fell in love with you tonight . . .

Sasha gasped, gripping her phone while giddily reading

the message over and over again. *Slow down, sis. Cool your jets.* She sent a lightweight response.

Lol go to bed, Mitch. And safe travels tomorrow. Chat soon.

Okay. But just know that I'm serious. Sweet dreams . . .

Sasha fell onto the bed and stared at the ceiling. She couldn't lie to herself. She was beyond flattered. But she was also in a relationship. Plus, there was a certain level of professionalism she needed to maintain with Mitch. This situation couldn't go any further. If a bit of flirting occurred here and there, so be it. But that was where the buck had to stop.

"And that's that," Sasha said, sauntering into the bathroom. But as she began her nighttime routine, she wondered whether she'd be capable of sticking to her declaration.

Sasha was sitting on the couch in her office at Kline & Associates, reviewing Mitch's On Bended Knee press schedule. A knock came at the door, and when it opened, Mitch came strolling in.

"Hey, you're early," she said, glancing down at her watch. "We're not supposed to get together until noon. And wasn't I going to meet you at the restaurant?"

"Yes, you were. But I'm starving. So I decided to come to your office in hopes that you could do something about that."

Mitch approached her and took the presentation from her hand. He knelt in front of her, and without saying a word, reached underneath her dress and removed her thong.

"Wait, what are you doing?" she gasped.

"Shhh. Just lay back and relax, baby. Let me take care of you."

Sasha wanted to protest. But the feeling of Mitch's warm, strong hands on her legs prevented her from speaking. He caressed them gently then pushed her dress all the way up. He leaned in closer, kissing and licking her thighs while opening them slowly. His tongue worked its way farther and farther up her legs, until finally, it fluttered over her clit.

"Oh, Mitch," she moaned. "We shouldn't be doing this."

Instead of stopping, Mitch grabbed her ass and squeezed it tightly. His tongue slipped deep inside her, and within minutes, she exploded in his mouth.

Sasha was still trembling when Mitch stood over her and pulled his thick long dick from his jeans. She took his erection in her hands and devoured it, running her tongue around the head and along the shaft before taking it all in.

Mitch slid his fingers between her legs and massaged her clit. His cock throbbed while her thighs trembled intensely. They were about to come together. But then, just as he grunted loudly, a nudge prodded her shoulder.

"Sasha. Sasha."

She let out a low moan, loving the way Mitch was calling her name.

Slowly, Sasha opened her eyes. And there, standing over her, was Drake.

She let out a yelp and shot straight up. Her gaze darted around the room. Her breathing quickened, and she struggled to figure out how she'd explain Mitch to Drake. But as her groggy vision became clearer, Sasha realized she wasn't in her office. She looked up at Drake in complete confusion. Then when she scanned the room again and saw she was at home in her bedroom, it finally dawned on her. She'd been dreaming.

"I don't believe this," she mumbled, rubbing her eyes then holding her head in her hands.

"Don't believe what?" Drake asked. "Are you okay?"

"Yeah. I . . . I'm fine," Sasha stammered. Sharp pangs of guilt stabbed at her gut. She could barely look at Drake after waking up from such a sexually charged dream, not to mention lying to him about last night.

"I've got good news," he said.

Sasha erased her sheepish expression before uncovering her face. She turned to Drake. He was sporting a crisp white shirt and navy slacks, and his hair was perfectly styled. It was the best he'd looked in weeks.

"What's up?" she asked. "Where are you off to?"

"Well, I finally took your advice and reached out to a few of my industry buddies to see if they knew of any job opportunities. Lee Sampson was the first person to reach back out. He worked as an assistant director on my movie *Deeper*, and he's about to start shooting an independent film in Ontario called *Rearview*. One of the actors just dropped out because his wife went into labor early. So the part is up for grabs. Lee thinks I'd be perfect for it."

"Oh, babe, that's awesome!" Sasha said, hopping up and throwing her arms around him. "I'm so happy for you."

"Hold on. Don't get too excited. It's just a small supporting role that isn't paying much. But the movie is a deep psychological thriller, and the script is phenomenal. So hopefully this part will at least get me back in the game. That is if I get it . . ."

"First of all, no role is too small at this point. And if you get the part and kill it, bigger and better offers will immediately start pouring in again. You'll be back on top in no time."

"Let's hope so. I really need this. Take it from me, being blackballed is no joke. It made me lose my motivation and confidence to the point that I didn't even wanna get off the couch. Being in front of the camera again would help get me back in fighting shape, both mentally and physically."

Seeing Drake like this swelled Sasha's heart. It had been quite some time since she'd seen determination in his eyes and a swagger in his demeanor. He'd lost all that after getting fired from *On Bended Knee*, along with his desire to be intimate with her, and vice versa.

In this moment, the attraction Sasha felt towards Drake sent heat seeping up her neck and a palpable vibration stirring between her thighs. She resisted the urge to pull him down onto the bed and have her way with him.

Drake glanced down at his watch. "I'd better get going. I wanna get to Lee's office early so I can run through my lines before I'm called in. Oh, and by the way, if I get the part, I'll have to leave soon. As in the next couple of days."

"Really? Wow . . . Well, we can handle it. Maybe some time apart would be good for us."

"Listen to you. Trying to get rid of me." Drake laughed, tickling Sasha playfully.

She shrieked and rolled over, struggling to push him away. He turned her back around and surprised her with a long, passionate kiss.

"Mmm." She sighed. "I miss that."

"So do I. We need to get back to it. Starting tonight. I'll plan a nice dinner, and afterwards we'll have one of our epic lovemaking sessions."

"That sounds wonderful. Can't wait. Now get outta here so you won't be late. I need to get moving, too. I'm presenting to a few of our new hires and I'm not totally prepared."

"Good luck with that. And hey, we'll talk about the trip to Cabo tonight, too. I know I haven't been contributing like I should. So let's go over everything and solidify plans together."

"I'd like that." Sasha smiled, glad to have the old Drake back. Seeing him like this made her want to tell him that she'd signed Mitch, because in spite of the rough patch they'd hit, she owed it to him to be honest. Plus, the last thing she wanted was for him to find out from someone else.

But now wasn't the time, considering Drake was on his way to an all-important audition. So Sasha decided she'd wait and share the news with him at dinner.

Then once that was out of the way, she'd figure out how to extinguish the latent desire Mitch had managed to ignite within her . . .

Sasha sped along the Pacific Coast Highway with her car top down and music blaring. The crisp ocean wind whipped through her hair while the setting sun warmed her skin. She readjusted her sunglasses and leaned back, relishing the moment. Sasha was happier than she'd been in quite some time. Life was good. As a matter of fact, life was great thanks to today, because everything had suddenly taken a turn for the better.

After she'd knocked her presentation out of the park that morning, Sasha received a text from Drake letting her know he had gotten the part. She'd screamed so loudly that Lori came tearing into her office, thinking something had happened to her. Drake then informed her he'd made dinner reservations at Hinata Sushi, the most exclusive restaurant in Malibu, and afterwards they'd check into the royal suite at The Malibu Oceanside, where they would spend the rest of the evening indulging in dessert and one another.

Sasha had something in store for Drake as well. That afternoon, she'd solidified plans for their Cabo vacation after deciding she would rather spend the evening reconnecting with him than coordinating the trip. She made some executive decisions on her own and created an elaborate agenda confirming the exact travel dates, resort location, and list of activities. Sasha sent the agenda to both sets of parents, and just as she'd expected, they got lost in the fancy presentation and agreed to everything.

She stopped at a red light and grabbed her phone, activating the voice-to-text feature then sending Drake a message asking whether he wanted to drive out to Malibu or arrange car service. She hadn't heard from him since early that afternoon, which was strange after they'd been communicating nonstop all morning. Sasha assumed he had gotten caught up in the whirlwind of preparing for his shoot and figured they'd hash things out when she got home.

She turned down her block and approached her house, expecting to see Drake's car parked outside. When she didn't, Sasha pulled into the driveway and tried calling him. She got his voicemail.

"Hey, babe, it's me. Tell Lee that he's going to have you all to himself in Ontario soon enough and you need to take a break to call your girl. But anyway, I just got home. Getting ready to freshen up and pack for our night. I'm so looking forward to this. Love you."

Sasha disconnected the call and practically floated inside the house. She set her tote down on the couch, then walked over to the closet to grab her suitcase. On the way there, she saw a printout lying on the bar. She picked it up and squinted while trying to make out exactly what she was looking at. Upon further inspection, Sasha realized it was a dark, grainy photo of her and Mitch, sitting in the booth at the Diamond VIP Bar.

Her stomach dropped to her knees. She trembled all over as beads of sweat formed along her hairline. Sasha held her breath, then read the blurb underneath the photo.

Our sly sleuths here at Gotcha! *strike again, this time catching powerhouse publicist Sasha Williams cozying up to A-list actor Mitch Morrison. Sasha, who's known for mixing business with pleasure, is also Mitch's new publicist. So does this mean it's a wrap for her and Drake Lancaster? Apparently so, making it Drake's second humiliating termination in recent weeks after he got booted from King Gary Rosen's latest blockbuster production,* On Bended Knee. *What's worse is that Mitch was hired to replace Drake on the film. Ouch! Will Sasha and Mitch make it down the aisle? Will Z-listed Drake go back to waiting tables?*

Stay tuned, as we here at Gotcha! *work to getcha all the latest scoop!*

Sasha leaned against the wall and slid to the floor. Tears streamed down her face. She looked down at the article again. A note from Drake was scribbled at the bottom.

Of all the guys you could've replaced me with, you chose Mitch Morrison? And I had to find out through some trashy blog? I thought we were better than that. Guess I was wrong.

Sasha balled the article up and threw it across the room. Her chest heaved with remorse. She sobbed for several minutes before grabbing her phone and dialing Drake again. The call went straight to voicemail. She hung up and sent him a text, apologizing profusely and asking him to please call her. Right when she hit *send,* a message came in from Nick.

In a meeting and can't talk, but I got a call from Drake saying he wants to sign with a new publicist, effective immediately. What's going on?

Sasha swallowed the bile that was creeping up her throat and struggled to steady her breathing.

"This isn't happening. This isn't happening," she said to herself over and over again.

She closed Nick's message without responding and sent Amanda a text, telling her she had an emergency and asking if she could come over ASAP.

Amanda replied immediately.

I'm on my way.

Sasha pulled herself up and poured a glass of wine, taking several quick gulps. *You can fix this.*

She took a deep breath and went into the bathroom. In between washing her face and brushing her teeth, Sasha texted Nick and explained that Drake was upset because he'd found out through a blog that she'd signed Mitch. She asked that Nick go ahead and assign him a temporary publicist until they worked things out. Within seconds, Nick replied.

Will do. I'll put him with Jonathon for now. Btw, glad to hear he's going to be a part of Lee's film. That's a good look. Drake told me Lee is bringing him on as a producer as well, so he flew to Ontario this afternoon to get a jump on things.

Sasha froze. Her phone slipped out of her hand. She must've read that wrong. Drake wouldn't have left town without telling her. But then again, considering that scathing blog post and Drake's accompanying note, he probably had.

Sasha felt as though she might faint. She doubled over, grabbing the vanity so not to fall to the floor. The doorbell rang, and she stumbled into the living room. When she opened the door, Amanda stood on the other side, and Sasha fell into her arms and sobbed uncontrollably.

Amanda managed to get her over to the couch.

Sasha laid her head on her shoulder and continued to cry while Amanda rubbed her back sympathetically. Once she was finally able to speak, Sasha told Amanda everything, then begged her to help fix things.

CHAPTER FIVE

Sasha exited the airport and climbed inside her awaiting car. She pulled out her phone and sent a text, confirming that she had landed and was heading to the hotel.

Sounds good. Glad you made it safely. I'll be leaving the set and heading your way soon. Meet you in the hotel restaurant?

Yes. See you soon.

Sasha glanced out the window, her hand against her chest in an effort to calm her frazzled nerves. She'd been through so much over the past several weeks. A few days after Drake had left for Ontario he'd finally called, and their conversation was nothing nice. They'd both hurled insults at one another for almost two hours. Drake accused Sasha of being a cheating liar while she fought to defend herself. She'd insisted that he had completely fallen off after getting fired from *On Bended Knee*, forcing her to carry their relationship alone. That was when Drake had lost it, swearing that she'd allowed Mitch to take his place both personally and professionally.

"Think about it!" she remembered Drake yelling through the phone. "I'm a white guy from the east coast who the entire industry has chewed up and spit out. Mitch, on the other hand, is the hottest thing in town, and he's got your undivided attention. You're both African-American, grew up in the same area, and the list goes on. How the hell am I supposed to compete with that?"

"It's not a competition, Drake," Sasha had fired back. "This is business, and Mitch is my client. That's it!"

"Then why did you lie to me about him?"

"I didn't lie. I just hadn't gotten around to telling you yet."

"You're so full of shit . . ."

The argument had ended when they hung up on one another with no resolution. And now, as Sasha stepped out of the car and entered the hotel, she had no idea where their relationship stood.

She checked in at the front desk and asked that they hold her luggage, then headed towards the restaurant. On the way there, Sasha's heart pumped erratically while her unsteady legs wobbled uncontrollably. She willed herself not to fall out. Just when she approached the hostess stand, someone called out to her.

"Sasha, hello there."

She turned around. "Hey . . . how are you?"

"I'm great, now that you're here," Mitch told her.

Sasha smiled and glanced down at her stilettos, not quite knowing how to respond.

"Welcome to New York. We've got a great table over by the window, overlooking the Hudson River. Shall we?"

"Yes, thank you."

Mitch offered Sasha his arm and led her to the table.

A fiery energy shot right through her at his touch. *Don't even start. Cut it out and keep it together.*

Mitch pulled Sasha's chair out for her, then sat and poured two glasses of wine. "Did I mention how happy I am to see you again?"

"No, I don't believe so."

"Well, I am. Let's make a toast. To successfully wrapping *On Bended Knee* as filming comes to an end, and to us. I can't wait to see what's ahead once I'm back in LA."

"And to this brilliant idea of hosting an early press junket," Sasha added, to deflect from discussing the two of them. "May it set the film off in the right direction, garnering plenty of critical acclaim and box-office moola."

"I'll drink to that."

She clinked her glass against his, then took a sip of wine. Mitch hadn't once taken his gaze off of her. Sasha's skin burned underneath the intense glint in his eyes. The moment was interrupted when the server approached the table.

After they'd ordered chopped salads, Sasha immediately went into publicist mode. She shared with Mitch all the plans she had for him once the movie wrapped. He fell right in line with the conversation, putting aside the flirtatiousness and offering up ideas as well.

Throughout their lunch, Sasha and Mitch kept the discussion tame. When they weren't talking business, they swapped stories about their college years and divulged hilarious family secrets. Being around Mitch reminded Sasha of home. Their similar backgrounds put her at ease, to the point that she felt as though she could tell him anything. And he effortlessly understood her, no lengthy explanations required. He just got her.

Before Sasha knew it, three hours had flown by. She drained her glass and sat back in her chair, watching while Mitch paid the check.

"Thank you for lunch." She smiled. "This was fantastic."

"You're welcome. It doesn't have to end here. We could take a walk along the river if you want, or what about dessert? I know a great bakery about two blocks away. They serve the best French pressed coffee and chocolate croissants."

"Tempting, but I'm really exhausted. I need to get some rest before the press junket and after party. I can't believe you're not tired, too, considering your crazy shooting schedule."

"I'm running on pure adrenaline, baby. My girl is in town. How can I sleep knowing I could be hanging out with you?"

"And on that note . . ." Sasha smiled, refusing to fall down Mitch's rabbit hole. "I'm going to head to my room. We'll reconvene in a few hours at the junket."

"Oh well, I tried," Mitch quipped, his gaze glued to Sasha when she stood. "May I at least walk you to your room?"

"Don't worry, I'm fine. You probably need to get ready for your prep meeting with the cast anyway, right?"

"That was a really slick way of getting rid of me." He laughed, following Sasha out of the restaurant. "But at least I get to see you again later on."

"Yes, you will. Hopefully I'll be well-rested and on top of my game."

"Of course you will be. Now go relax, beautiful."

Mitch moved in closer and embraced Sasha, then took her head in his hands and kissed her on the cheek. His warm, soft lips lingered for several moments.

Sasha didn't realize she'd been holding her breath until she almost choked.

"Are you okay?" Mitch asked, gently caressing her back.

"Yep, I'm good," she sputtered, anxious to grab her luggage and get to her room before she gave in to Mitch's seductions and did something she'd regret. "I'll see you later."

Sasha hurried towards the lobby. She couldn't deny the chemistry between them. But in spite of that, she also couldn't seem to keep the thought of Drake out of her mind. Sasha really did miss him. But considering they weren't even on speaking terms, she had no choice but to focus on work, which at this point was a welcome distraction.

"To the cast, crew, and everyone who's been a part of this film," Gary Rosen said, his glass raised in the air, "I thank you from the bottom of my heart. I know a hit when I see one, and we've got a monster on our hands, baby. Here's to *On Bended Knee* being a smash at the box office!"

"Cheers!" the crowd exclaimed, toasting with their glasses and hugging one another.

Everyone was gathered in Gary's massive suite, and the after party was in full swing. When the DJ turned the music back up, several people bum-rushed the makeshift dance floor that had been set up in the middle of the living room. Sasha and Mitch were chatting with a group of his costars, who were spilling on-set secrets about who was sleeping with whom and which actors didn't get along.

Sasha grabbed Mitch's shoulder and leaned in closely. "I just might be a tad bit tipsy." She giggled.

"Well, I just might be flat-out drunk." He laughed.

"Oh no! What're we gonna do?"

The DJ switched to a mid-tempo song, and Mitch took Sasha's hand in his. "We can hit the dance floor and show everybody how it's done, Chicago-steppin' style."

"Ooh, yes, let's get it," Sasha replied, letting Mitch lead the way. She hadn't stepped in years, and the smooth, foot-shuffling style of dance had been taught to her by her parents.

Couples on the dance floor cleared the area and watched in awe as Sasha's and Mitch's bodies moved together seamlessly. They stepped towards one another then two-stepped back, dipped down and spun around, then started the moves all over again. By the end of the song they'd worked up a sweat and received a round of applause.

One of the executive producers of *On Bended Knee*, who'd clearly had one too many, stumbled towards them. "I don't know if the rumors about you two are true or not," he slurred loudly, "but you all seem perfect for one another. Can you teach me how to do that dance?" he asked, swaying back and forth so hard he almost knocked himself down.

"Maybe later, Harry." Mitch laughed. "When you're steadier on your feet."

"You just don't want me to show you and your girlfriend up," Harry replied, winking at Sasha and staggering off.

"Your *girlfriend*," Sasha said to Mitch. "Is that what these people think I am to you?"

"Well, you heard all those reporters at the press junket, didn't you? They were so busy asking about us that I barely had a chance to talk about the movie."

"Yeah, I noticed. I was going to just ignore it, but it seems as though the rumor is taking on a life of its own."

"Why don't you hold off on releasing any sort of statement for now, and let's see how things play out between us?" Mitch suggested, staring at her intently.

Before she could respond, Gary approached them. "Wonderful job on the junket, Sasha. Let's meet when I'm back in LA. I'd love to collaborate with you on some upcoming projects I've got in the works."

"That would be fantastic, Gary. I'll have my assistant reach out to your office once filming wraps."

"Wonderful. Looking forward to it," Gary replied, turning to Mitch. "Hey, I've got a couple of investors here who're looking to break into the film business, and they wanna meet you. Come find me when you and Sasha are done, and I'll introduce you."

"Awesome, I'll be over in a sec," Mitch said.

Once Gary was out of earshot, Sasha turned to Mitch with raised eyebrows. "Well, look who's officially made it onto the Rosen team. Good job. You're definitely in there now."

"One can only hope," Mitch responded humbly.

"Go ahead and meet the investors. I'm gonna call it a

night and head up to my room. I've got a super early flight back to LA in the morning."

"Nooo, come on. You can't leave now. We're having such a great time!"

"I know, but it's so noisy down here, and I'm beat. Plus, I cannot miss my flight. I've got several meetings that would be impossible to reschedule."

"I'll tell you what. Let me go meet these investors and chat with them for five minutes. Ten tops. After that, I'll head up to my suite where it's nice and quiet. You meet me there so we can have one last nightcap and say a proper goodbye."

Sasha side-eyed Mitch. "What do you mean by *a proper goodbye*?"

"Woman, get your head out the gutter." He laughed. "I legit just wanna say goodbye to you without all the madness and people around."

"No funny business?"

"Of course not! Unless that's what you want . . ."

"Boy, you'd better stop with all that." Sasha pointed, giggling when Mitch grabbed her by the waist.

"I'll be good. I promise."

"Fine. I'm going to go change into some jeans and sneakers. Text me when you're done, and I'll stop by and have one drink. *One.*"

"Cool. But don't get mad when we're alone and you decide you can't keep your hands off me."

"Just text me when you're done," Sasha said, waving Mitch off and heading to her room.

Once there, she slipped out of her dress and heels then decided to take a quick shower. After she slathered her body with perfumed soap, she grabbed her razor and shaved her legs, even though she'd just shaved a few hours ago.

Sasha got out and dried off, then massaged scented lotion

into her skin, spritzed her pulse points with her favorite perfume, and slipped on a skimpy black lace thong and bra. That was when it dawned on her. She was subconsciously preparing to do way more with Mitch than just have a nightcap. And in that moment, she decided she was fine with it.

Right when Sasha pulled on her jeans and a cropped sweater, her cell phone buzzed. It was Mitch, letting her know he was back in his suite and waiting for her. She replied.

Be there in a sec.

An arousing anticipation simmered deep within her.

Sasha darted into the bathroom and retouched her makeup, then freshened her curls with serum.

Just as she was walking out the door, her phone buzzed again.

"Stop being so impatient!" She giggled aloud, assuming Mitch was texting her to find out what was taking so long. But when she opened the message, it wasn't from Mitch. It was from Drake.

Sasha stopped dead in her tracks. She quickly clicked on the notification, eager to find out what he had to say.

Hey. I've been thinking about the trip to Cabo and wondering what we should do. My parents keep asking about it. As far as they know it's still on. What do you want me to tell them?

Sasha had been avoiding the subject of their vacation because she had no idea how to handle it. She hadn't told her parents that she and Drake were having problems, so as far as they were concerned, the trip was still happening.

Sasha asked what *he* wanted to tell them, but his response surprised her.

I've been so wrapped up in filming that I haven't really thought about it. My parents have never been to Mexico, and they're really stoked about the trip. I don't want to disappoint them.

Sasha replied.

Same here. My parents haven't been to Mexico either, and this trip is all they've been talking about.

Drake responded.

Well, I'm still down to go if you are . . .

Sasha's mouth fell open, and she held her hand to her chest. She read Drake's message over and over again, her eyes filling with tears as her heart filled with hope. That was the last thing she'd expected to hear from him. She'd been fully prepared to have to cancel the trip and leave everyone disappointed. She replied.

I'm still down to go.

Okay, cool. We wrap next week, and I'll be back in LA. Maybe we can meet up for coffee and finalize plans then.

Sasha exhaled, choking back tears while typing.

I'd like that. Looking forward to it.

Right when she hit the *send* button, Mitch messaged her.

Did you forget about me? The champagne and I are getting lonely up here.

After that message exchange with Drake, Sasha's desire to

hang out with Mitch had suddenly fizzled. She wrote back.

Hey, sorry. I think I may have indulged in one too many cocktails at the party. Mind if I call it a night?

Not at all, beautiful. I'll take a rain check. Get some rest.

Thank you. Goodnight.

And with that, Sasha removed her makeup, took off her clothes, and slipped into bed. Her mind raced with a slew of possibilities for her and Drake.

Pump the brakes, sis. She needed to manage her expectations. But when she closed her eyes, Sasha couldn't help but ponder her and Drake's future.

Sasha was sitting out on the patio of the Santa Monica Sip, frantically stirring the ice in her macchiato while tapping her feet underneath the table erratically. She turned around and stretched her neck once again, then glanced down at her watch. Drake should've arrived over twenty minutes ago. She checked her phone to see whether he'd called or texted. He hadn't. *I know this man isn't standing me up.*

When she looked up from her cell, Drake headed her way. All eyes were on him as he walked through the crowd, waving and speaking to his fans and stopping for a few selfies. Ontario had clearly been good to him, considering how great he looked. Gone were the extra pounds he'd put on after getting fired from *On Bended Knee*. He was ripped, clean-shaven, and appeared every bit the quintessential superstar.

Sasha stood as Drake approached the table, and they greeted one another with an embrace. She closed her eyes and inhaled his fresh scent, every tense muscle in her body easing in his arms. His touch made her realize just how much she'd missed him. But before she could really relish in the moment, Drake pulled away abruptly and slumped down in a chair across from her. She sat slowly, watching while he removed his sunglasses, yawned, and rubbed his eyes vigorously.

"How are you?" she asked. "Tired?"

"Very. I flew in really late last night and didn't get much sleep."

"Well, how about ordering a coffee to perk you up? I can't wait to hear all about how shooting went on *Rearview*, then we can go over the plans for Cabo."

"Actually," Drake said, checking his phone, "I don't have much time. I've got a post-production meeting starting soon, so we need to make this quick."

"Oh . . . um . . . okay," Sasha stammered, her smile fading. "I was hoping we'd have some time to talk, but . . ."

"My mom mentioned some agenda you sent detailing all the plans. Did you email that to me?"

Sasha stared at Drake with a blank expression, wondering why he was being so short with her. "I did. Weeks ago." She reached inside her tote and grabbed an agenda. "But I brought you a copy just in case you hadn't seen it."

Drake took the paper and glanced over it. "Yeah, well, I've been so inundated with this movie that I haven't had a chance to do much else."

"I can imagine. I've heard some really great things about it so far. And by great, I mean Oscar-worthy-performance great."

"Really?" Drake muttered, his gaze still glued to the agenda.

"*Yes*, really!" Sasha's tone heightened as she leaned into the table. "Wouldn't it be crazy if *Rearview* ends up getting you a golden statue? That would mean being fired from *On Bended Knee* was a blessing, since you never would've even considered taking such a small part prior to that."

Drake finally looked up at Sasha, his expression riddled with irritation. "Yeah. That would be crazy," he deadpanned.

"Wait, that came out all wrong. I'm sorry." She reached out and tried to touch Drake's hand, but he pulled away quickly.

"Don't worry about it," he huffed, pushing the agenda across the table, then standing. "I need to get going."

Sasha sat back in her chair in utter defeat, willing herself not to cry.

"Oh, and by the way," he continued, "I saw the pictures of you and your boyfriend Mitch dancing together at Gary's party all over the blogs. Glad to see things are working out so well for you two."

"Drake, Mitch is not my boyfriend. We were just—"

"I know, I know. You were just dancing, right? Funny how everyone else seems to think otherwise, including Mitch."

"I'm telling you the truth, Drake. There's nothing going on between Mitch and me."

"That's not my business anymore," he responded coolly, slipping on his sunglasses. "See you in Cabo."

And with that, Drake turned around and walked off.

Sasha closed her eyes and counted to ten in an effort to stave off the panic attack coming on. Once her breathing settled, she got up and left, struggling not to burst into tears before making it to her car.

CHAPTER SIX

On Saturday morning, Sasha decided to take a much-needed sleep-in day. Between hustling for work and being rebuffed by Drake, she had no desire to do anything except lie in bed and catch up on her DVR'd television shows.

She grabbed her phone and pulled up the *News Now* blog, then clicked on the entertainment section. The first thing that popped up was a photo of Drake and Lee on the set of *Rearview*. The mere sight of him felt like a physical blow to her heart. She scrolled down and read the blurb.

We here at News Now *have placed our bets on Lee Sampson and actor-producer Drake Lancaster sweeping this year's awards season with their upcoming film,* Rearview. *Even the toughest of critics are calling this psychological thriller a masterpiece thanks to an exquisite script, first-rate director, and superb cast. Needless to say, Drake Lancaster is officially back. We can't wait to see what this dynamic duo will deliver next.*

Sasha was stunned. She thought back on the moment Drake had woken her from that dream she'd had about Mitch and told her he was auditioning for this movie. She'd figured it would help get him back in the game. But she had no idea that small role would catapult him further than he'd been prior to being fired by Gary.

As Sasha continued reading, a video chat request appeared on the screen. She immediately accepted it without paying attention to the caller's name, thinking Drake was reaching out to ask about Cabo. But when Mitch came into view, her expression fell.

"Hey, you. Did I catch you at a good time?"

"Hey, sure, now's fine," Sasha said, trying not to sound as disappointed as she felt. "What's up?"

"I took an unexpected trip to San Francisco last night to meet with Gary and those investors who were at the party in New York. They really want to be a part of his next film, but only if I'm attached. Can you believe that?"

"Actually, yes, I can. You're winning everyone over, Mitch. Your agent and I can barely keep up with all the calls and emails we're getting. Everyone wants you in their next project or at their event. You're in high demand right now, so ride the wave and enjoy it. You deserve it."

"Thank you, thank you. I'm definitely enjoying it. But this would all be so much sweeter if I had you by my side, taking it all in with me."

"Oh, Mitch . . ." Sasha sighed, not quite knowing how to respond.

"Oh, Mitch what?" He smiled. "Come on, girl. You can't deny what's happening between us. We've got so much in common, we have a ton of fun together, and we make a great team. We'd make the perfect power couple, wouldn't we?"

"I've kind of got a situation going on already," Sasha finally admitted to him. "And it's complicated."

"Well, since you still owe me a rain check after our night in New York, why don't you tell me all about it over dinner tonight? I'm flying back to LA this afternoon. We can—"

"Mitch, I can't," Sasha interrupted, her chest tightening as tears stung the corners of her eyes. "My heart is elsewhere, and at this point I'm just not ready to jump into anything."

"Let me guess. Drake Lancaster?"

"Yes," she whispered.

"I thought you two were done."

"I honestly don't know what we are. But I still care about him, and I owe it to myself to sort it all out before getting involved with someone else."

"Okay, I understand," Mitch replied, his low tone filled with disappointment. "I guess I shouldn't be too broken-hearted, since I've still got myself a great publicist and a great friend."

"Yes, you do. And I've got myself an extremely talented client and great friend as well."

"I just hope Drake realizes what he's got and treats you right."

"Actually, Drake and I aren't really on speaking terms right now, which is odd considering we're about to take a trip to Cabo with our parents. To celebrate Valentine's Day, no less."

"Uh, yeah, that's definitely odd. Why aren't you two speaking?"

"Because I did something stupid. Back when I signed you, I didn't tell him about it, trying to spare his feelings since you'd replaced him in Gary's movie. Well, that backfired, and Drake found out about it through a blog. Then he saw pictures of us online at the Diamond Bar, dancing at Gary's party, and it just wasn't a good look."

"But nothing's going on between us. That meetup at the Diamond Bar was just an introduction, and us dancing together at the after party was perfectly innocent. Now had you come to my room to the *after* after party that night, maybe it would've been a different story, but . . ."

Sasha and Mitch both laughed before he continued.

"If your heart is still with Drake, he needs to know that, and you two should try and work things out."

"Easier said than done. His ego and pride are standing in the way. But we'll see. At least he's got what looks to be a hit movie on his hands. And maybe being away from LA and on a beach in Cabo will help clear his head so that he can hear me out."

"Well, good luck with that. You're my girl, so I'm rooting for you. I just wanna see you happy."

"That's really sweet of you, Mitch. Thank you."

"With that being said, you got any cool girls you can hook me up with?"

"As if you need help meeting women." Sasha laughed. "I'm sure you do okay all by yourself."

"I don't like to brag, but, you know, what can I say? I'm kidding. Anyway, I'd better get outta here before I miss my flight. Maybe we can get together for lunch after your trip and catch up."

"I'd like that. I'll call you when I get back. Safe travels."

"Same to you. Good luck with your boy."

"Thank you," Sasha said before disconnecting the call. She laid her head back and closed her eyes, grateful she'd cleared the air with Mitch and hoping she and Drake could somehow work things out.

"Welcome to Playa del Bonita, senorita," the bellman said after Sasha's driver opened the door. "May I please take your bags?"

"Yes, you may, thank you."

She had just arrived in Cabo, and the serene, beautiful beachfront surroundings did nothing to calm her anxiety. No amount of meditation, wine on the plane, or reassurance from Amanda could convince her that this trip wasn't going to be a total disaster.

"Good afternoon, Miss Williams," the reservations attendant said when she approached the front desk. "We've already processed your online check-in, and your suite is ready. Here's your key, and here's a resort pamphlet and

Wi-Fi instructions. Please call us or the concierge anytime if you need assistance."

"Thank you."

"Oh," the attendant continued, "and the rest of your party has already arrived. Mr. and Mrs. Doug and Sharon Williams, Mr. and Mrs. Stan and Dolores Lancaster, and Mr. Drake Lancaster. They told me to please let you know they're out by the pool enjoying taco and tequila hour, and to join them when you arrive. I'll have the bellman take your bags up to the room if you'd like."

"That would be great, thank you."

"You're welcome, Miss Williams. Enjoy your stay."

Sasha headed to the ladies' room to freshen up. She tried to ignore the nauseating Valentine's Day décor that was hanging everywhere. After reapplying her lipstick and fluffing her hair, she took a deep breath and headed out to the pool, hoping for the best but expecting the worst as the bougie Lancasters faced off against the downhome Williamses.

The minute she walked out onto the gorgeous deck, a loud cackle erupted that had her mother's name written all over it. She made a sharp left turn. Her parents sat at a table across from the Lancasters. Drake was standing over his mother's shoulder, his arms flailing while he spoke animatedly. Whatever he was saying had the whole group in stitches.

Sasha slowly headed towards the table, shocked at what she was seeing. Drake's mother and her mom were leaning into one another, patting each other's arms and nodding in unison. The dads were sitting back laughing up a storm, waving their wives off and high-fiving one another.

So all it takes is a little sunshine and a few shots to unite polar opposites. Duly noted . . .

"Is that my baby?" her mother yelled.

"Yes, it is!" Sasha exclaimed, hurrying over and hugging her mom tightly.

"You look gorgeous, honey," Sharon continued. "Come on, let me show you off to everyone. Oh, and by the way," she whispered, "that man of yours is *fiiiine.* You done good, girl."

"Calm down, Mom." Sasha smiled tightly, her heartbeat bumping erratically when she realized Drake was staring at her. "Hello, everyone," she said, giving her father a big hug.

"Hey, baby," he boomed. "It's so good to see you."

"So," Drake's father said, "you must be the infamous Sasha Williams our son's been talking about incessantly." He shook her hand warmly. "It's a pleasure to finally meet you. I'm Stan, and this is my wife, Dolores."

"It's a pleasure to meet you both as well," Sasha said, managing not to make eye contact with Drake.

Dolores stood and greeted her with a hug. "Hello, Sasha. My goodness, you're pretty in pictures, but you're stunning in person. And this hair!" She reached up and ran her fingers through Sasha's curls. "It's so luscious. How do you get your coils so defined?"

"Okay, Mom, that's enough," Drake interjected, walking over and taking her hand in his.

"What? What'd I do?" Dolores asked, looking around at everyone with wide, innocent eyes.

Sasha glanced over at her mother and saw the expression of death on her face. They held back laughter, knowing they were both thinking the same thing. Touching an African-American woman's hair without permission was a no-no.

"Hey, Stan, why don't we go order another round of tacos and tequila?" Doug asked.

"I'll drink to that," Stan agreed.

"I think you've had enough," Dolores chimed in. "But when in Cabo . . ." She sat back down at the table and sipped her drink.

Sasha's mother joined her, and the fathers headed over to

the bar. Sasha and Drake were left standing next to one another, acting as though they were complete strangers until he finally spoke up.

"Hey."

"Hey."

"You uh . . . you look great," Drake told her.

Sasha turned to him, surprised he had something nice to say. "Thanks. So do you."

His gaze darted around the pool before he turned back to her. "So, uh, our parents seem to be getting along well. They've only been here for about an hour or so, but they're already having a blast."

"Good. I'm glad. That was the point of this trip, wasn't it?"

"It was. Partly. The other point was for us to spend some time together, away from the LA spotlight and drama."

"Yeah, well, we don't have to worry about that leg of the trip, so . . ." Sasha suddenly teared up. "You know, I haven't been up to my room yet, so I'm gonna go get settled since everything seems to be okay down here."

Before Drake could respond, Sasha hurried off, letting their parents know she'd rejoin them a little later. She then rushed inside the lobby, barely making it onto the elevator as she burst into tears. *This was a mistake. I never should've have come. This is too much for me.*

Sasha's minded flooded with thoughts of negativity. She contemplated whether she should head to the airport and go back home. Then she figured she was just tired and needed to lie down. Either way, Sasha realized she felt better being away from Drake and not having to act like she wasn't bothered by their situation.

Sasha entered her suite and went straight into the bathroom, taking a cold, damp towel and laying it across her forehead. Then she grabbed a bottle of water from the mini fridge, turned on the television, and lay across the bed. The minute she felt herself drifting off to sleep, there was a knock at her door.

"Damn it," she muttered, climbing out of bed. Sasha figured it was her mother, wondering why she'd run off. But when she opened the door, Drake was standing on the other side.

"Oh. Hey. I thought you were my mom."

"Nope. It's me. Can I come in?"

Sasha opened the door wider and stepped to the side. She hoped he wasn't there to argue, because she just didn't have it in her.

Drake walked through the living room and stood over by the sliding glass doors, staring out at the ocean.

"I owe you an apology, Sasha," he said, shoving his hands down in his pockets then turning around and facing her.

"You do? Why?"

"Because I accused you of something that wasn't true. And I didn't believe you when you tried to explain yourself to me. For that, I'm sorry."

"*Okay*," Sasha replied slowly, her gaze darting around the room in confusion. "Where is all this coming from?"

"Actually, Mitch. He called me. And he explained that you two are just colleagues and friends. Then he sang your praises and told me how lucky I am to have you, and that he hopes I'd be willing to give us another chance."

"He *did*? Wow," Sasha uttered, shocked by what she was hearing. The fact that Mitch was able to put his feelings for her aside and talk to Drake proved that he really was a great friend.

Drake sauntered over to her, removing his hands from his pockets and wrapping his arms around her. "So do you accept my apology?"

"I do. And I want to apologize to you again. I'm sorry I

didn't tell you I'd signed Mitch. I called myself trying to protect your feelings, since it was such a sensitive situation, but ended up making things much worse. And I shouldn't have lied to you about meeting with him at the Diamond Bar. That was wrong of me."

"It was. But I accept your apology, and I'll acknowledge my part in that as well. I'd really fallen off during that time and had gotten away from myself. I wasn't being a good boyfriend, either. So I get it."

Sasha laid her hands on Drake's chest. "Thank you. I really appreciate that." She paused, then took a deep breath and continued. "So now that we've both accepted each other's apologies, where do we go from here?"

"Where do you want to go?"

"I asked you first," Sasha rebutted before they both broke out into laughter. She felt as though a fifty-pound weight had been lifted off her back, and being in Drake's arms had never felt so good.

"Full disclosure?" Drake asked, leading her over to the bed. "I wanna go all the way."

"Oh, do you now," Sasha replied, unbuttoning his shirt while he unzipped her dress.

They wasted no time undressing each other and lying down, kissing and caressing one another hungrily.

"You have no idea how badly I've wanted to taste you," Drake said, taking her breasts in his hands. He swirled his tongue around her nipples then sucked and bit them until they hardened.

"I wanna feel you." Sasha moaned, grabbed Drake's ass, and shoved him between her legs. "All of you. *Now.*"

"But I'd rather tease and punish you with extended foreplay after you've been so naughty," Drake said devilishly.

"I think not," Sasha shot back, rolling her hips until Drake's dick slipped inside her.

"Babe!" He groaned. "*Ahh . . .* why'd you do that? I wasn't ready!"

Sasha locked her legs tightly around his waist so he couldn't pull out. "Because *I* was ready. And as you can see, I get what I want."

"Of course you do." Drake panted, his slow strokes accelerating as his thrusts intensified.

Sasha pushed him over onto his back and climbed on top. She gradually slid his cock deep within her then swayed her hips in arousing circles.

"Girl, what are you doing to me?" he howled, gripping her thighs while their bodies moved in sync.

Sasha responded by reaching back and taking is balls in her hand, massaging them with her fingertips. Then she reached down with her other hand and slid her fingers around the base of his cock, squeezing gently.

"Wait . . . Sa . . . *Sa . . .*" Drake sputtered, his body slowly convulsing.

Sasha quivered, throwing her head back and letting out a low whimper. "I'm about to . . ." Her voice trailed off, and they came together.

Sasha fell onto Drake's chest. They struggled to catch their breath while holding one another tightly.

"I'm mad at you," he insisted. "I wasn't ready to come. You owe me another round."

"Shouldn't we go back down to the pool and check on our parents?"

"Probably, even though I'd rather stay in bed with you."

"We've got plenty of time for that," Sasha murmured, planting soft kisses on Drake's earlobe and neck.

"You'd better stop before you awaken the sleeping giant again," he warned before rolling over. "Come take a quick shower with me."

"If I do that we'll never make it outta here."

"Yes, we will. I promise."

Right when Drake stepped out of bed, his and Sasha's phones buzzed simultaneously. They grabbed them, then looked at one another.

"It's my parents," they said in unison.

Sasha laughed and opened her message. "So apparently the tacos and tequila got the best of our guests. They're exhausted and heading up to their rooms to rest."

"Yeah, that's what my mom's saying, too." He glanced over at Sasha with a devilish grin. "You know what that means, don't you?"

"Round two?"

"Indeed!" Drake dove back into bed and grabbed hold of her.

"You have no idea how much I missed this," she told him. "And you."

"Ditto," he said, pulling her in closer. "I love you, Sasha Williams."

"I love you, too, Drake Lancaster."

"Oh, and by the way? Happy Valentine's Day."

"Happy Valentine's Day, baby."

Sasha held Drake's face in her hands and kissed him passionately. In that moment, she realized he was her one true, unconditional love. And she made a promise to herself to never take that love for granted again.

You may also enjoy the following from eXtasy Books Inc:

Shadow of a Man
Denise N. Wheatley

Excerpt

Veronica Level opened her eyes and blinked rapidly. She struggled to clear her blurred vision as she slowly came to. When she was finally able to focus, she gasped at the horrifying scene in front of her.

The smoldering air was filled with thick gray smoke. Cars were piled on top of one another all along the expressway. Horns were blowing, sirens were blaring. Terrified people were jumping out of their burning vehicles, running and screaming. The crowded, five-lane highway had suddenly turned into an apocalyptic warzone.

Veronica gripped her steering wheel and turned around, afraid of what lay behind her. Just as she'd thought, there was more mayhem. Dark clouds loomed overhead. Dozens more overturned cars littered the street, many of them engulfed in flames. She carefully reached for her door handle, hoping that she hadn't broken any bones. Despite feeling shaken and drained, Veronica felt no pain.

She opened the door and stepped outside, bracing herself

for the damage that her own car must have sustained. But as Veronica eyed her driver's side, she saw that there was none. Shocked, she rushed around to the passenger side. It too was unscathed. She looked up and saw a bloody man limping toward her, his face distorted in agony as he struggled to support what looked to be a broken right arm.

"You all right?" he heaved.

"Yes, I think so . . . Are you okay?"

"I will be, but I don't know about my wife. She's unconscious. I'm trying to flag down a paramedic." The man looked over at Veronica's car. "There's no damage," he uttered in disbelief. "How in the hell did you manage that?"

"I uh . . . I have no idea . . ."

Veronica turned her head to hide any hint of deceit glimmering in her pale green eyes. She did in fact have an idea as to why her car hadn't been damaged. But she certainly couldn't share that information with a total stranger. Or anyone else for that matter.

Unbelievable . . . Veronica heard the man thinking to himself. How the hell is this woman and her car in pristine condition when the rest of us are out here practically dying? It's unreal. This isn't fair.

Veronica stared at the stranger sympathetically. It was happening again. Just as it always had during intense moments of danger such as this.

The man began looking around frantically as his breathing quickened. Where's the help? he asked himself. We need help! What if Susan dies? And the kids. How will I explain all this to the kids?

"Your wife is going to be fine," Veronica divulged abruptly. "So you won't have to tell your children a thing. Trust me, she'll be fine."

The man stared at Veronica. "Wait, but how did you know that I was even—"

"Is everyone all right over here?" a paramedic asked as he rushed toward them with a medic kit in hand. "Do either of you need assistance?"

"I do!" the man exclaimed, forgetting about Veronica and her cryptic premonition. "My wife, she's still in the car, and I don't know if she's . . ." The man's voice broke.

"Just show me the way, sir," the paramedic said, helping the man walk back to his car. "I'll do whatever I can to save her."

Veronica felt for him and his family. She watched as he limped away, still hearing thoughts of worry flying through his head. Her ability to read minds was still just as powerful as it had ever been. It was a skill that she'd possessed since early childhood. And while she had never really been fascinated by her telepathic ability, it was a phenomenon that her aunt Samantha considered to be a great gift, while her mother, Amanda, had deemed it a freakish curse.

Aunt Samantha always thought of herself as a clairvoyant of sorts, as did Samantha's mother, her mother's mother, and on back through the generations. Samantha's sister Amanda, however, tried to break the chain early on and refused to tap into any sort of psychic abilities that she may have possessed. The last thing Amanda wanted was to be deemed a weirdo by her peers, unlike Samantha, who relished in her telepathy despite being ostracized by their classmates.

During high school, Amanda couldn't help but be embarrassed by Samantha's tendency to accentuate her round baby-face and sinewy figure with dramatically colorful makeup, teased, fiery red hair and flamboyant, gypsy-like clothing. As a result, Amanda felt compelled to downplay her flowing blond locks and pretty, delicate features with simple chignons and modest, classic makeup and attire. The last thing she wanted was to draw even more unwanted attention to the family.

Through the years, Samantha always felt as though her niece, Veronica, possessed a sixth sense that enabled her to see, hear and feel things beyond the average person's capabilities. So the day she discovered that Veronica actually did have the ability to read minds, she was absolutely elated.

It happened one chilly fall evening when Veronica was in the second grade. Samantha had taken her to the local grocery store to pick up last minute Halloween candy. Even though Amanda insisted that they had enough candy and should've gone out earlier while it was still daylight, Samantha dismissed her, saying that she was overreacting as usual.

Samantha and Veronica went to the market against Amanda's wishes and headed straight to the candy aisle, stocking up on several bags of chocolates and fruity treats. They checked out and walked back through the parking lot toward Samantha's car. On the way there, Veronica noticed two big, burly men dressed in all black, lurking in the back of the lot.

Veronica stopped in her tracks. "Auntie Samantha, look!" she pointed, her finger trembling as her eyes widened.

"Come on, Vee, let's go!" Samantha insisted, grabbing Veronica's little hand out of the air and pulling her along. "If we don't hurry up and get back we'll miss the trick-or-treaters!"

Veronica stumbled behind Samantha reluctantly, scowling at the men in the distance.

This is gonna be easy, she heard one of the men say. But when she looked out at him, he was too far away for her to see his face, let alone hear his voice. All's I gotta do is stick to the plan. I'm grabbin' the kid, Carlos is grabbin' the old bitch, we throw them both in the van then speed off. No sweat.

Veronica squinted, watching fearfully as the men began to walk toward them. Their jumbled thoughts continued to buzz around in her head. Suddenly, it dawned on her that she wasn't hearing the men's voices through her ears. She was hearing their thoughts through her mind.

Veronica stopped again and squeezed Samantha's hand urgently. "They're gonna get us," she whispered.

Samantha stopped and frowned at Veronica. "What are you saying, child?"

"If we go to the car, those men are going get us."

"Look sweetheart, Auntie is in a hurry. Not only do we need to get back for the trick-or-treaters, but my favorite true-crime show comes on in a few minutes. If I miss one second of it, I'm going to be very upset with you."

"Auntie Samantha, I heard them. They said they're gonna throw us in the van and take us!"

Samantha looked at Veronica in dismay and sighed. "Those men?" she pointed, "All the way over there? Honey, how could you even . . ."

About the Author

Denise N. Wheatley has been a lover of storytelling for as long as she can remember. She cried as a three-year-old child when her mother read to her because she so badly wanted to read the books herself. Once she learned, she constantly had her nose in a novel. Denise holds a degree in English and is in love with love, romance and happy endings. She's published several books and short stories, and is an avid ghostwriter, editor and blogger. When she isn't sitting behind her computer, you can find Denise in a movie theater, on a tennis court, watching true crime television or chatting on social media.